P9-CFJ-838

AWARDED BY THE INTERNATIONAL BUREAU ON BOOKS FOR YOUNG PEOPLE ✱ MEINDERT DE JONG FOR THE MOST DISTINGUISHED CONTRIBUTION TO INTERNATIONAL CHILDREN'S LITERATURE 1962

First American Winner of the International
HANS CHRISTIAN ANDERSEN AWARD

NOBODY PLAYS WITH A CABBAGE

NOBODY PLAYS
with a
CABBAGE
by MEINDERT DEJONG
Winner of the 1955 Newbery Award
Pictures by Tom Allen

Jim Jordan's family was so helpful with Jim's vegetable garden that there was nothing for Jim to do. But he was willing to wait. And indeed, his family soon lost interest in the slow-sprouting seeds, and Jim's garden became really his.

Then suddenly it looked as though there would be no garden, for there was nothing left except one tiny plant. But even one small cabbage can make a garden if you are willing to help. And Jim was willing.

As the summer progressed, the cabbage grew bigger and healthier. A toad and a snail made their homes under its broad leaves, and a young rabbit lived nearby. Jim watched and waited and worked, and the summer went on.

Meindert DeJong, known and loved for his understanding and sensitivity, has written a story young readers will take completely to heart. For it is a success story, a story which proves that if you want something hard enough, and love it, and work for it, it will be yours.

Books by Meindert DeJong

ALONG CAME A DOG

BILLY AND THE UNHAPPY BULL

THE CAT THAT WALKED A WEEK

DIRK'S DOG BELLO

GOOD LUCK DUCK

THE HOUSE OF SIXTY FATHERS

HURRY HOME, CANDY

THE LAST LITTLE CAT

THE LITTLE COW AND THE TURTLE

THE MIGHTY ONES

SHADRACH

SMOKE ABOVE THE LANE

THE TOWER BY THE SEA

THE WHEEL ON THE SCHOOL

NOBODY
PLAYS
WITH A

HARPER & ROW • PUBLISHERS • NEW YORK AND EVANSTON

CABBAGE

by Meindert DeJong

Pictures by Tom Allen

NOBODY PLAYS WITH A CABBAGE
Copyright © 1962 by Meindert DeJong
Printed in the United States of America

Library of Congress catalog card number: 62-7586

For my brother, Neil, who was this way—his own young way —when we were very young

About Meindert DeJong

Meindert DeJong was born in Wierum, a Frisian village in the Netherlands, and came to the United States when he was eight years old. The DeJong family settled in Grand Rapids, Michigan, where he grew up and was educated.

In 1962 Mr. DeJong was the first American to be awarded the Hans Christian Andersen Medal by the International Board on Books for Young People. This organization, made up of fifteen member nations and concerned exclusively with children's literature, was founded in 1956, with headquarters in Zurich, Switzerland. Believing that good books for the young stimulate the cause of humanitarian education and training and promote international friendship, the IBBYP presents its award every two years. The award was given to Mr. DeJong for the entire body of his work (over twenty books), rather than for a single book.

Mr. DeJong was nominated for the award by the Children's Services Division of the American Library Association.

CONTENTS

THE BIG SIGN SAID

There was this boy who had a garden, and the garden had a big sign. The boy's name was Jim— Jim Jordan was his name. The sign said so. The big sign said:

JIM JORDAN'S VEGETABLE GARDEN

It wasn't Jim who had given the garden the big sign, and the big name. It was his sister, Julia. She had the idea. She liked to letter and make signs. Julia liked to make signs with big black letters and big red letters. She did it for school, and she did it for fun.

Jim's big brother, Harold, liked the sign Julia had made. He also liked to hammer and saw and nail. He made a frame for the big sign. It was as neat as a picture frame. Harold covered the sign with transparent plastic to protect it against the wind and the sun and the rain. He nailed the sign to a thick, sharp-pointed stake. He drove the stake into the ground in

1

a corner of the backyard. It was a corner, between the garage and the neighbor's high fence, where nobody ever went.

There stood the sign in the corner where nobody ever went. Now the sign said it was:

JIM JORDAN'S VEGETABLE GARDEN

But what the sign said wasn't true, because there was no garden behind the big sign.

Jim took his mother by the hand to show her the

big sign in the corner. Jim's mother immediately hurried to the store to buy vegetable seeds. She bought corn, she bought beans, and carrot and broccoli seeds—she even bought little cabbage plants in the store. And she bought Jim a small hoe and a rake and a cultivator. They came in a package with a cellophane cover.

Jim's father came home that evening, and drove the car up to the garage, and almost up next to the big sign in the corner, before he saw the sign, and Jim and his mother waiting for him at the sign. From the car Jim's father read out loud from the sign:

JIM JORDAN'S VEGETABLE GARDEN

He laughed, and asked, "But, Jim, where is this garden that the sign is shouting so loudly about? Those letters are red in the face from shouting."

Jim's mother said, "Don't laugh. There's not only the sign, but there are seeds, and cabbage plants. And here are Jim and I waiting for you to help change this corner into a vegetable garden."

Then Jim's father jumped right out of the car and ran to the garage to fetch the spade.

While Jim's father was still spading the little garden Harold and Julia came home hungry for supper, but they had to help with the garden, too. "Nobody gets supper," Jim's father said to them, "until we've made this vegetable garden."

Harold had to rake the garden soft and smooth

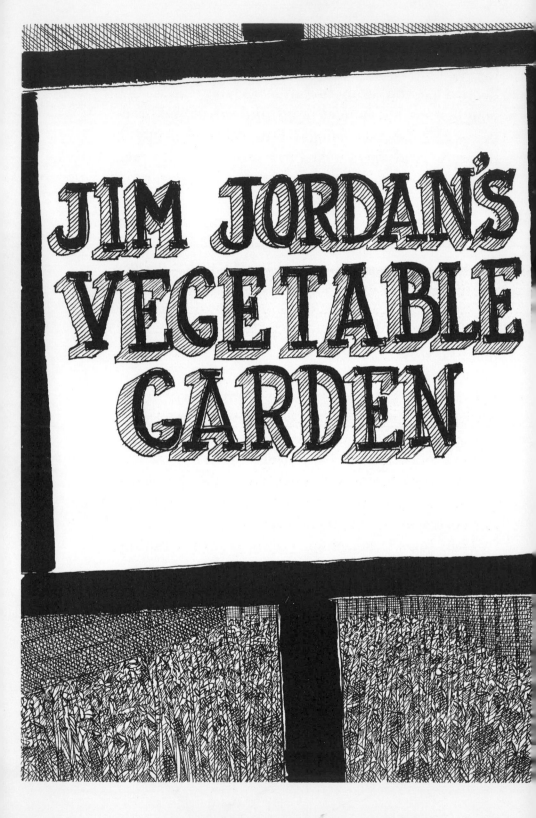

JIM JORDAN'S VEGETABLE GARDEN

for the little seeds. Then Jim's mother planted the seeds, Jim's father set out the cabbages, and sister Julia put the empty seed packages on little sticks at the end of the rows to show just what was going to come up in the rows.

There were far too many cabbage plants for such a small garden in such a small narrow corner between the garage and the neighbor's fence, so Harold took the left over cabbage plants to the neighbor's chickens to eat. Then Jim's father raked the garden smooth again from all their footprints and scuff marks, and they were done.

The garden was done, and they all went into the house to their supper.

In the house, around the supper table, everybody talked about the new garden. Harold leaned across the table and said to Jim, "Jim, I'll hoe your garden every day. I'll keep the weeds down between the rows."

"Oh, well, then I'll pull up the weeds that come up *in* the rows," Julia said excitedly.

"Well, that doesn't leave much for me to do—it's such a little garden," Jim's mother said. "But I'll water the garden every day—except when it rains."

"Well, now—well, now," Jim's father said. "That doesn't leave much of anything for me to do, does it, Jim? But I'll promise you I'll keep a stern eye on everything to see that they do what they're promising you."

Nobody thought that this didn't leave anything at

all for Jim to do for his garden. And there were the hoe and the rake and the cultivator side by side in the package with the cellophane cover.

At his place at the table Jim did not say anything about the hoe and the rake and the cultivator. He just smiled at all the excited talk, but he said nothing. What could he say? He did not know about gardens, so what could he say? He said nothing. And there were the hoe, and the rake, and the cultivator side by side in the package under the cellophane.

THE LITTLE HOE WAITED

It was a long, long time to wait for a garden. Every day Jim went to his garden to sit with his legs crossed under him, and his back propped up against the stake of the sign to wait for his garden. The big sign was there, the cabbage plants were there, but there was nothing else, except the empty seed packages on their little sticks. The pictures on the seed packages showed great big leafy, round, tall plants of beans, carrots, corn and broccoli—but that was on the seed package signs, they weren't in the garden.

Oh, at first Jim did not wait alone. At first everybody came to the garden. They did not sit and wait with their backs propped up against the stake of the sign, but they did come to look.

It was a long, long time to wait. And then they didn't come to look at the garden any more. At supper time around the table they didn't talk about the garden any more. It was a long, long time to wait, and side by side in the package with the cellophane

7

cover the little hoe and rake and cultivator waited—because there was nothing to do but wait.

Then the weeds came up! The weeds came up before the corn and carrots and beans and broccoli came up. They came up all over the little, narrow garden. They came up between the rows, and in the rows—they even came up among the cabbage plants.

Jim waited. But Harold did not come to hoe the weeds between the rows as he had promised. Harold was busy building a tree house in a tree in somebody else's yard. Jim took off the cellophane cover of the

package, and took out the little hoe, and hoed between the rows.

Julia did not come to pull up the weeds that came up in the rows as she had promised. Julia was busy making big signs for the whole school for a school carnival. Jim pulled up the weeds that had come up in the rows.

It wasn't easy to know what to pull up in the rows. Jim did not know about little corn and bean and carrot and broccoli plants—he could not tell them from the weeds. And the pictures on the seed package signs showed only big, grown, leafy, tall, round plants. Jim looked at the back of the seed package signs, and on the back of the seed package signs there were little pictures of two-leafed little plants the way they looked when they first came up out of the ground.

Now Jim knew what to do. He held the seed package sign between his thumb and finger. With his other thumb and finger he pulled up every plant that did not look like the two-leafed plants on the back of the seed package sign. He held his eyes close to the picture on the seed package sign, and his eyes and his nose close to the rows, and he pulled up all the weeds in the rows.

It was all weeds, for when Jim was done there were no bean and carrot and corn and broccoli plants in the rows—they still had to come. And the garden that had been a garden of weeds now was a garden of dirt again—except for the row of cabbage plants.

Then Jim took out the rake and the cultivator from the package with the cellophane cover, and he raked the garden smooth again, exactly the way he had seen his father do. He raked out all his own footprints and scuff marks. His father had gone out of town on a business trip, he *could* not keep a stern eye on everything as he had promised Jim. So Jim kept a stern eye on everything.

But then there even came a day—after a day when it had rained—that Jim's mother became so busy that she quite forgot to water the garden after the day when it had rained. Jim dragged the hose to the backyard and watered the garden.

The sign said:

JIM JORDAN'S VEGETABLE GARDEN

And now it really was Jim's garden, because he did everything for his garden.

One evening, with all the weeds pulled and all the work done, just before his bedtime Jim was sitting under the sign before his garden—there in a smooth spot the ground began to crack—the ground broke open. A BEAN came up!

The bean hunched its round back, pushed up with its little round back—and there came the bean! There it stood with its little bent stem in the sun! But the little brown bean up on top of the stem split itself open to the sun, and inside the bean were two tiny leaves. The two tiny pale leaves opened themselves to the sun. And the sun loved the bean, and the bean loved the evening sun. Jim Jordan stormed to the house to get his mother—to take her by the hand and show her the bean with its little pale leaves opened to the evening sun.

Then it was night and sleep and darkness, and Jim slept in his bed in the house. But the beans that had slept in the ground for so long did not sleep this night. In the night all the beans in the row pushed their round backs up through the ground, and when Jim came to the garden in the morning there stood the beans all in a row in the

sun, and the little pale leaves spread themselves to the morning sun.

The next night in the sleep and darkness the corn came up through the ground. In the morning there was a row of sharp little spears of corn—like a row of green spears of little green soldiers. The little spears seemed to march on behind the big sign.

On another night the broccoli plants came, and much later came the row of carrot plants with their ferny leaves. The garden was full. What the big sign said was true—there now was the vegetable garden!

That day Jim Jordan pulled up the sticks with the seed package signs. For now he did not need the seed packages any more to show him how the little two-leafed plants would look when they came up from under the ground. He knew how they looked, he knew it by heart.

But the big sign stayed, and said in big letters:

JIM JORDAN'S VEGETABLE GARDEN

IT WAS TOO LATE

Then there came a night, and another night, and there came a morning when awful things began to happen to the garden.

The first night a dog came. The dog liked the soft, deep spaded ground of the garden in the corner between the garage and the fence. To the dog it seemed just the right place to bury the big bone he was carrying.

The dog did not know about beans and carrots and corn and broccoli—the dog just knew about bones. He buried his big bone in the broccoli row. He dug a hole with his paws—and the dirt flew and the tender little broccoli plants flew. Then he buried the bone and he covered the bone—with dirt and with broccoli plants.

Another dog came the same night. He sniffed and snuffled along the broccoli row—he smelled the buried bone. He dug it up to steal it, and again the dirt flew and the tender broccoli plants flew, and the dog went away with the bone.

13

All in one night there was nothing left of the broccoli row. There was no more broccoli in the morning.

The second night two cats came to the garden. Night came, and some cat chased another cat into the garden in the corner—and they fought. They grabbed each other and picked up each other and hurled each other against the fence, and against the garage, and against the big sign. The big sign did not go down, but the tender, ferny carrot plants went down as the cats bit and clawed and screamed and rolled over and over the carrot row.

It was such a fierce screaming fight in the night, it woke everybody up in the house. Everybody sat up in bed. Upstairs in his bed Jim sat listening wide-eyed to the wicked sounds of the wicked fight in his garden. Downstairs Jim's father stumbled out of his bed, stumbled sleepily out to the porch, picked up an old shoe from the porch and hurled it in the night.

Maybe the shoe hit the high fence and bounced back in the garden. Maybe it hit the sign and tumbled over the sign into the garden. Maybe it even hit the two cats rolling over and over each other in the carrot row. Maybe it did, maybe it didn't—who can tell in the night?

But in the morning the tender, ferny carrot plants lay crushed and torn, and smashed and scattered. And some lay on top of the cabbage plants, and some hung wilted from the cabbage plants. But in the middle of the cabbage plants—heel up, sole up, and upside down—there lay the big, black shoe.

In the morning after the fierce cat fight the whole family went out before breakfast to look at the garden, and there lay the ferny carrot plants—scattered.

"Oh, what a pity," Jim's mother said.

That is what they all said. "What a pity, Jim. What a pity."

The whole family stood there, but they all just looked. Nobody could seem to do anything but look. Nobody even picked up the old, black shoe that lay in the cabbage row. It seemed no use.

"All the work we did on that garden and now the whole garden is practically gone," Julia said. "What a pity!"

"It's a dirty shame," Harold said. "And the way I worked and hoed and raked—all for nothing."

But Jim's mother held Jim close.

"It *is* a pity, and it *is* a shame," Jim's father said angrily. He was angry with the dogs and the cats, but mostly he was angry with himself. "I should

have thought of cats and dogs," he said angrily. "I could have kept them out of the garden. Why, there's a roll of chicken wire in the garage, and if I'd only thought—why, we could have stretched the chicken wire across the front of the garden, and nothing could have got in. If I'd only thought—but I guess none of us know very much about gardens. But next year, Jim, next year we'll do it better, next year we'll put up the chicken wire, and then you'll have a garden all fenced in."

"No, now," Jim said. He looked at the big sign, and then he said it again, "NO, NOW."

"Then, NOW!" Jim's father said, still angry with himself. "Right here and now—before anybody gets any breakfast."

Everybody helped with the chicken wire—to unroll it and stretch it and hold it while Harold wired the chicken wire to the neighbor's high woven-wire fence, and Jim's father nailed the other end of the chicken wire to the corner of the garage.

"Now, look, Jim," his father said. "I won't nail the bottom of the chicken wire to the garage—I'll just drive some nails in part way, and bend them for hooks. Then you can unhook the bottom of the chicken wire from the bottom nails to let yourself into your garden. You can let yourself in, you can let yourself out, but nothing else can get in—not a dog, not a cat, NOTHING!"

There stretched the tight chicken wire across the front of the garden, and it looked so safe, they went into the house to have breakfast. But Jim first had to try the chicken wire. He unhooked and then he carefully hooked the bottom of the chicken wire around the bottom nails, and it looked so safe, he, too, went in the house to have breakfast around the big table with his father and mother, and sister and brother.

But somehow during breakfast the neighbor's chickens got out of their coop. The neighbor's chickens had never been outside before. They went wild with delight. They ran and they flew in the neighbor's big yard under the big, free sky. They flapped their wings and tried to fly. One of the chickens even tried to fly up into the big, high sky. It could not fly that high—it could only flutter as high as the fence. It fluttered and tumbled over the fence into Jim's garden. Then all in a storm of squawkings and cacklings and feathers and wings, the whole flock flew after the first chicken into Jim's garden.

In the house around the breakfast table they heard the chickens squawking, and they all ran out. Jim's father outran them all. He ripped the bottom of the chicken wire from the bottom nails, and he dived under the wire into the garden—headfirst and head-long. The scared chickens rose straight in the air, they exploded into the air. In a wild storm of squawk-ings and feathers and wings, they flew over the fence, back into the neighbor's yard. But it was too late—the chickens had eaten everything.

Harold and Julia ran to tell the neighbor, and they tried to help the neighbor shoo his chickens back into their coop. Jim's father picked himself up. From behind the chicken wire he looked down at Jim, and helplessly said, "Next year, Jim, we'll even put chicken wire *over* the garden! We'll roof the garden with chicken wire, so that not even a chicken can get in." But now it was too late.

Jim's mother kneeled down in the dirt, and held him close, and said, "Yes, next year—next year, Jim." But now it was too late.

Then, what with fixing the chicken wire across the front of the garden before breakfast, and chasing the chickens out of the garden after breakfast, it was so late everybody had to rush and hurry and run.

Jim's mother had to hurry into the house to get school lunches ready. Harold and Julia had to stop running after the chickens in the neighbor's yard. They were so late, they had to grab their lunches and run to school. Jim's father was so late he had to

jump in the car and rush away. But Jim crawled under the chicken wire and went into the empty garden.

The chickens had eaten everything. There was nothing left in the garden, except the shoe. The neighbor was still shooing the chickens back into their coop. But Jim stood looking down at the old shoe.

THE NEIGHBOR KNEW

At last the neighbor had all the chickens shooed back into their coop. He locked them in. He came to the fence. He was panting. He looked through the high woven-wire fence at Jim.

Jim did not look at the neighbor. He bent way down and looked at the shoe.

"Yes, Jim, I understand," the neighbor said sadly.

Jim did not say anything. He wanted to cry. There was nothing left in the garden except a row of the stumps of the beans, and the stumps of the cabbage plants. The corn was gone—the chickens had pulled up and eaten the corn. There was only the shoe. Little Jim bent way down and looked at the shoe.

The neighbor looked at the shoe. "What can I do, Jim?" the neighbor said. Jim did not know what to say; he did not know what to do. And because he did not know what to do, Jim picked up the old, upside-down shoe.

22

"What can I do, Jim?" the neighbor started to say again.

But Jim said, "LOOK!"

"Imagine!" the neighbor exclaimed. "One little leftover cabbage plant! One little cabbage saved from the greedy chickens by the shoe!"

And they both looked at the cabbage plant—it was a little bit crushed.

"One cabbage plant," the neighbor said again. "Well, it isn't much, and it's a little bit bent, but maybe—just maybe, Jim, you and I can make a garden of it yet with just one cabbage plant. Maybe we can grow that little cabbage plant into a big, prize cabbage that'll all but fill your little garden. I know about gardens and cabbages, and I'll tell you what to do."

And Jim looked at the neighbor.

"Listen, Jim," the neighbor said. "You pull up all the stumps of cabbage plants, and all the stumps of beans and put them around the little cabbage plant. Then they, too, in their way will help to make the cabbage grow into a big, prize cabbage. And while you do that I'll get you a sprinkling can and box of fertilizer as a gift for what my chickens did."

Jim pulled up the little stumps, and made a soft bed of bean and cabbage stumps around the one leftover cabbage that had been saved by the shoe.

Over the fence the neighbor made Jim a present of a green sprinkling can. "It's just the right size," the neighbor said. "And every day you pour a sprinkling can of water around your cabbage, and all over the little bed of stumps. It will make the little stumps softly melt into the ground to become part of the ground that will make your little cabbage grow into a big, prize cabbage."

Then over the fence the neighbor made Jim a present of the box of fertilizer. "Now you must be careful with that fertilizer," he slowly, carefully said. "You must sprinkle the fertilizer around your cabbage only about *once* in every *four* weeks."

Jim slowly nodded his head.

"Yes, but, Jim," the neighbor said, "you won't know when four weeks are gone again, so I'll tell you. Every time the moon gets full, and shines full in your upstairs bedroom window, then four weeks are over again. So the very next morning—after the night when the moon is full—you must give your cabbage a sprinkling of that powdery fertilizer out of the box."

Jim listened carefully, and he slowly nodded his head.

"But you mustn't give it too much," the neighbor warned. "You must give it only as much—well, only as much as the sugar you sprinkle on your cereal in the morning. Can you do that?"

Jim nodded and nodded and nodded. Oh, he liked that! And he liked the neighbor, in spite of what the chickens had done. The neighbor had told him just what to do, but he was going to let him—Jim—do it!

The neighbor looked at his watch, and said, "Oh, now I'm late for work!" And the neighbor ran.

Then Jim ran. He ran to the house to get his mother and show her the one lone cabbage.

FEATHERS FOR A CABBAGE

The big sign said:

JIM JORDAN'S VEGETABLE GARDEN

But there was only the lone, little cabbage in the garden and the old shoe that had saved the cabbage. Jim carefully put the shoe in the back of the garden against the garage and the wooden back fence— in the corner where the one cat had cornered the other cat, and where they had fought. Jim carefully laid the big shoe on its side, so it wouldn't fill up with rain.

Then there was this one cabbage and it grew and grew in its soft, moist bed of bean and cabbage stumps and chicken feathers. For Jim even had picked up the feathers the chickens had left behind when his father had dived headlong into the garden, and the scared chickens had exploded out of the garden—he had given them all to his cabbage plant.

26

With the sprinkling can Jim watered the bed of stumps around the cabbage every day—even on days when it rained. He did more. For as the little stumps softly began to melt into the ground to become part of the ground that grew the cabbage, Jim searched the whole yard every day for fallen leaves from trees, and tufts of grass that grew in corners, and weeds he pulled up from under bushes—and he gave them all to the cabbage plant.

Sometimes little feathers of birds floated down into the yard—Jim also gave those to his cabbage. The weeds and leaves and tufts of grass made a bed for the cabbage plant. But the chicken feathers and the colored feathers of little birds, made the bed look almost like a nest for a lonely little cabbage plant.

Every four weeks—every time the moon was full in his upstairs bedroom window—Jim carefully watched to see exactly how much sugar he sprinkled over his cereal. Then after breakfast—after the night when the moon was full—he would sprinkle exactly that much powdery fertilizer around his cabbage plant.

But four weeks were so long that sometimes in between the four weeks, Jim brought his cabbage a spoonful sprinkling of *real* sugar. The neighbor had not said to give the cabbage sugar, but it was nice to do and four weeks were so long.

It all was nice to do—hunt the leaves, and search for feathers, and give the cabbage sugar. It was fun.

It was sort of a game that was fun. It was almost as if Jim were playing with his cabbage. Of course, nobody plays with a cabbage—Jim was growing the cabbage!

Then the cabbage wasn't little any more. The cabbage began to spread its big, flat leaves as if they were green wings it held out to the sun. The cabbage began to rise on its straight, thick stem, as if to rise up to the sun. There it stood big behind the big sign.

The big, broad leaves began to spread themselves out toward the garage and the neighbor's fence. The broad leaves even spread themselves out toward the old, black shoe in the corner—as if they wanted to shade the shoe that had saved the cabbage!

But one day two leaves at the top of the cabbage did not spread themselves broad and flat. The two little top leaves curved and curled themselves toward each other—as if they were trying to trap the sun— as if the cabbage wanted to tuck the sun inside itself.

More leaves came and curled themselves over each other, and made themselves into a loose, green ball. The green ball at the top of the cabbage became as big as Jim's fist.

But the whole cabbage with its spreading leaves was so big the little garden did not look empty any more. The big sign said:

JIM JORDAN'S VEGETABLE GARDEN

It was as if the big cabbage was trying to fill the whole garden to make what the big sign said true.

THE SNAIL AND TOAD STAYED

In the following days a snail came to the cabbage. The snail came in the night—slowly in the long, slow night. It found a wilted cabbage leaf lying on the ground under the cabbage. The snail was so slow, it took the snail the whole long night to nibble and softly crawl its way around the edge of the wilted cabbage leaf. When the morning came, and Jim came to the cabbage in the garden, there was the snail hidden under the fallen cabbage leaf.

Jim saw the silvery trail that the snail had left. He lifted the leaf. There was the snail all sleepy slow. The snail was silver—so all soft silver, it even left a silver trail.

Little Jim was glad the snail had come to the cabbage. Now the cabbage did not seem so lonely any more. Jim decided that if the snail would stay, he would even break off a bottom leaf from the cabbage for the snail after the wilted leaf was gone and had melted into the ground.

29

The snail stayed.

In the following days a toad came to the cabbage. It did not come in the night like the snail—it came in the day, for it had come for the night insects that hated the sun and hated the day, and hid from the sun under the dark, cool cabbage leaves. Mosquitoes hid there. The toad flicked out its swift little tongue, and flicked the mosquitoes away.

The snail had not hurried away when Jim had come to the cabbage. The snail could not hurry. But when Jim saw the toad, and pushed his head under the bottom leaves of the cabbage to see what was

under the cabbage, the toad hopped away. It hopped from under the cool, dark cabbage, and sat in the sun. Its little heart beat, its sides pounded, and its little eyes bulged.

Jim stretched out his hand, and pulled the toad out of the sun back under the cabbage, for Jim had found to his surprise that is was nice under the cabbage. Under the cabbage it was cool and moist, and under the cabbage was a cool, moist smell—the way the whole earth smells after the rain.

But under the cool cabbage the toad's little heart pounded away just as hard as it had in the sun. Its sides beat against the inside of Jim's hand. Its eyes

bulged out to see right before it a boy's big head that was ten, eleven times bigger than all of the toad was itself.

Jim did not know what to do for the toad. But he thought of the neighbor's dog that liked to have its back stroked and petted. Then Jim stroked the toad the way he stroked the neighbor's dog—except with just the tip of one finger—it was such a little back.

It was a knobbly back! Jim was surprised. The toad wasn't cold and wet and sticky—the toad's knobbly back was cool and dry. You couldn't stroke a snail—a snail was all soft silver, but you could stroke a knobbly toad. A toad was cool and dry!

Then Jim was even more surprised. The toad liked to be stroked! Maybe the little toad was even more surprised than Jim, but its heart and its sides didn't pound so hard any more. Oh, its eyes still bulged, but they bulged from pleasure at being stroked. Then Jim let go of the toad. It did not hop away into the sun. It stayed under the cabbage near Jim's head. And they were friends.

They stayed friends. In the following days the day even came when a mosquito flew down from under a cabbage leaf to the tip of Jim's nose under the cabbage. But just as the mosquito bit and stung, the toad flicked out its swift little tongue, and flicked the mosquito away. They were friends under the cabbage. And under the cabbage it smelled the way the whole earth smells after the rain, and the toad stayed under the cabbage.

THE WREN AND THE RABBIT

In the following days the top leaves of the cabbage kept curling and curving into a bigger and bigger green-leaf ball. The green ball of cabbage wasn't as big as Jim's fist any more—it was bigger. Jim thought it was easily as big as his head. Well, as big as a doll's head, he thought, as big as a big doll's head.

But in the following days, over the high woven-wire fence and over the high chicken wire butterflies fluttered down to the cabbage. Some were all

white, some were all yellow, and some had tiny blue polka dots. They fluttered all over the cabbage, and laid eggs on the head and the leaves of the cabbage. The eggs became little green caterpillars—as green as the cabbage. The green caterpillars ate the green cabbage. They ate and ate, and that made them bigger, and the bigger they became, the more they ate. Jim did not like them, but he did not know what to do about them.

There was this wren. It was busy, busy, busy. It was all busy, busy all the time building a nest in the tree that grew before Jim's upstairs bedroom window. In the day the leaves of the tree hid the nest. But on the nights that the moon was full, Jim could look through his bedroom window and see the wren on its nest in the tree against the yellow moon.

The little wren had built its nest, and now it was sitting on eggs. It sat very quietly for such a busy wren, until there were four baby wrens in the little cup of a nest up in the tree. Then the mother wren was busy, and busier than ever again. It had four wide-open mouths of four baby wrens to feed.

There were the baby wrens, and there was the cabbage. The mother wren found the big cabbage. The high fence and the chicken wire did not stop the wren. It sailed from the tree to the top of the fence, and hopped from the fence to the cabbage. Here was a cabbage, and there was the tree with four hungry baby wrens in the nest. Here were the caterpillars on the cabbage. Back and forth, and back and forth from the cabbage to the tree the mother wren flew —each time with a caterpillar in its quick, busy bill.

Jim came to the cabbage in the garden to look for the snail and to stroke the toad. When the little wren flew down from the tree to the top of the fence there was a boy with his head under the cabbage. The little wren on top of the fence scolded Jim. It seemed to say, "Get away, boy—get from under that cabbage. I'm too busy, busy, busy to sit on a fence waiting for you."

The bold little wren was even too busy to sit there

and scold. The brave, bold wren darted down to the top of the cabbage, scooped up a caterpillar, and swooped up to the nest in the tree. It was back in a moment. It had no time to bother with a boy with his head under a cabbage. It hunted all over the cabbage for caterpillars, whispering busy little whispering things to itself about a nest full of wrens, a cabbage full of caterpillars, and a boy with his head under a cabbage.

The little wren was wonderful. For there was the cabbage and it grew and grew, because the mother wren kept the caterpillars from eating the cabbage. But up in the nest in the tree were four baby wrens, and they grew and grew from the caterpillars on the cabbage. Down in the garden the cabbage grew, up in the nest the little wrens grew—it was a wondrous wonder!

In the following days a baby rabbit came to the cabbage. It came on a night when the moon was full, and that was how Jim saw the rabbit come to the cabbage.

Jim was sitting up in bed looking out through the window and the tree to see if the moon was full, and if it was time again to give his cabbage a sugar sprinkling of powdery fertilizer in the morning. The moon was full. The whole yard was white and bright with moonlight. Even the garden in the lost corner next to the garage was light and the top of the big cabbage was glossy green with moonlight.

Then tearing across the moonlit yard came the

rabbit. And howling right on behind the rabbit came a big hound. The scared little rabbit dashed everywhere in the yard, under the bushes and into the corners, but the howling hound came right on behind. The little rabbit did not know where to turn any more. It dashed across the whole yard—it dashed right at the chicken wire that was stretched across the front of the garden. Up in his bed Jim Jordan was so scared for the scared rabbit, he could not even yell out—his throat was closed.

Amazingly, the little rabbit did not dash itself up against the chicken wire—it squeezed *under* the wire! It scooted under the shadowy cabbage.

Up in his bed Jim Jordan laughed, for now he remembered he had forgotten to hook the bottom of the chicken wire around the bottom nail in the garage. He had! He had forgotten! He laughed and laughed, for the big hound dashed himself against the stretched chicken wire—he was too big to squeeze under. The stretched, tight chicken wire threw the hound back. With a loud, surprised WOOF the hound bounced back from the chicken wire, and lay in the yard, legs kicking the air. Jim laughed.

The dazed hound picked himself up. And he must have thought that the rabbit had dashed through the fence into the neighbor's yard, for the hound did not throw himself up against the chicken wire a second time—no, he climbed the neighbor's high woven-wire fence! He pulled himself up by his paws, he tumbled himself over the fence, he picked him-

JIM JORDAN'S
VEGETABLE
GARDEN

self up, and howled away into the night.

But the trembling rabbit sat in the safe, dark shadows under the spreading leaves of the moonlit cabbage. The hound howled away. The rabbit was safe. The cabbage had saved the rabbit!

Amazingly, the baby rabbit was still under the cabbage when Jim came to the garden in the morning. The little rabbit did not stay under the cabbage. It was almost as scared of Jim as it had been of the howling hound in the night. It dashed to the back of the garden to get as far away from Jim as it could. But then when it did not know where to turn any more it dived into the big, black shoe!

The baby rabbit was so small it could easily dive into the shoe that lay on its side in the corner. But the little rabbit trembled so hard inside the shoe it shook the shoe, and the shoe trembled. Jim did not know what to do for the scared rabbit. He thought that maybe if he gave the rabbit a big breakfast of a cabbage leaf, the little rabbit would feel better. He broke a big bottom leaf off the cabbage for the rabbit, and quietly went away. He forgot to hook the bottom of the chicken wire around the bottom nail in the garage on purpose. If after the big breakfast of a cabbage leaf the little rabbit would feel braver and better it could squeeze under the wire and be on its way.

Jim waited on the steps of the front porch. And, oh, it was long to wait, for he hadn't yet looked under the cabbage for the snail, and he hadn't yet stroked the knobbly toad. He hadn't even given the cabbage its sugar sprinkling of fertilizer—and last night the moon had been full! But the rabbit had come.

At last Jim went back to the garden. The little rabbit seemed gone. Even the leaf Jim had broken off for the rabbit was gone. But when Jim looked in the corner, the cabbage leaf wasn't gone—it had gone into the shoe with the rabbit. The rabbit had pulled the cabbage leaf into the shoe; it was nibbling

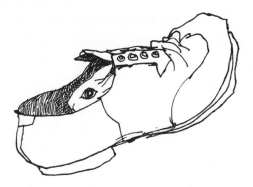

the cabbage leaf in the shoe. The whole shoe wiggled from the quick, busy nibblings of the rabbit, and the tip of the cabbage leaf wiggled out from the shoe.

The cabbage was wonderful! The cabbage had saved the rabbit, and now the baby rabbit was eating a cabbage leaf inside the shoe that had saved the cabbage. It was wonderful.

Jim decided that if the rabbit wanted to stay, he would break a big bottom leaf off the cabbage for the rabbit every day. A big leaf like that would be a whole meal for such a small rabbit. The cabbage was so big, and the rabbit so small, the cabbage would not miss the bottom leaves at all. Why, the big cabbage could easily feed a baby rabbit and a whole nest of baby wrens, and still be a home to a snail and a toad!

The rabbit stayed with the cabbage.

Still the big cabbage grew. The green-leaf ball at the top of the cabbage grew. The ball that had been as big as a big doll's head was now bigger than Jim's own head. Why, Jim thought, even bigger than that! Bigger than his *father's* head—bigger and harder and tighter and crisper and, of course—GREEN.

NOBODY PLAYS WITH A CABBAGE

All this time in the house around the big supper table Jim's father and mother, and sister and brother puzzled about Jim and his garden with the one cabbage. Around the table they talked and talked among themselves, and guessed and guessed, and asked and asked each other questions.

Harold often asked, "Why is Jim always messing around in that old corner with one old, sprawled-out cabbage?"

Sister Julia asked again and again, "Whatever does Jim find to do in that little garden with just one big cabbage?"

Jim's mother would try to answer them. She'd tell them, "If Jim likes to be there, it's still his garden, even with just one cabbage. He's bothering nobody, and he's never out in the dangerous street. You're not home all the day, but it's nice to know where Jim is almost all the day—he's in his garden."

Then after *they* talked and asked and guessed and guessed, Jim's father would sometimes say, "Jim, if you so like to play in that corner shall I put up some boards, and bring in a load of clean sand for a sand box?"

But Jim would shake his head. What could he say? What could he tell them?

He couldn't say, "I like to play there with my cabbage."

Nobody plays with a cabbage.

And Jim guessed that at night around the supper table they liked to talk, and guess and guess, and ask each other questions. It was fun for them. But he liked to play with the cabbage—it was fun for him. But you couldn't say, "I play with a cabbage."

Nobody plays with a cabbage! All a cabbage does is grow.

That is exactly what the cabbage in Jim's garden did—it grew. But while it grew it fed the baby rabbit and the baby wrens, and while it grew it was a home to a knobbly toad and to a snail that was soft silver.

Then in the following days there came a day when the little rabbit no longer needed the cabbage and the shoe. The baby rabbit had grown from eating the leaves of the cabbage. It had grown too big to hide in the shoe, but it had also grown fast enough to outrun anything—even the fastest howling hound.

On that day before he went to bed Jim forgot— on purpose—to hook the bottom of the chicken wire around the bottom nail in the garage. That night the rabbit squeezed under the chicken wire and was on its way.

In the following days the little white and yellow and polka-dot butterflies did not flutter down to the cabbage any more. They did not lay eggs on the cabbage any more. Soon there were no caterpillars on the cabbage for the little wrens. But the baby wrens had grown big from the caterpillars on the cabbage —big enough to fly anywhere. The day came when they flew with their mother to the South—to the cabbages and the caterpillars in the warm South.

Here it was getting cold. Fall was coming, the nights were sharp, and the days windy. One windy

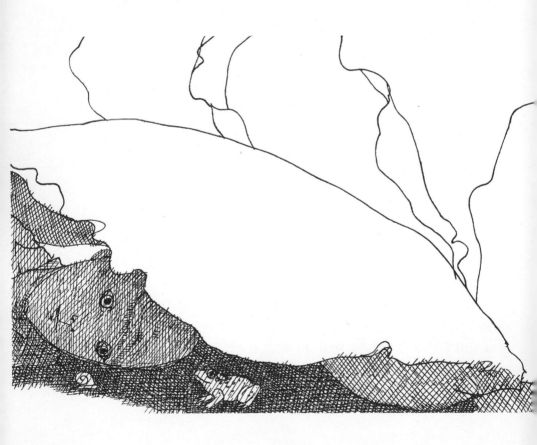

night the empty nest of the wrens blew out of the tree that grew before Jim's window. In the windy morning Jim picked up the fallen cup of a nest, and gave it to his cabbage. It seemed right and nice to give the nest to the cabbage that had fed the baby wrens in the nest.

Jim put the nest under the cabbage upside down. It made the upside-down cup of a nest look like a little, strawy, Eskimo igloo. That day the slow snail crawled into the wren-nest igloo. And because the Fall and the cold and the wind had come, the snail stayed under the upside-down nest. No longer did the silver snail crawl about, leaving its silvery trail.

In the afternoon of the windy day the toad dug itself a little hollow in the soft ground under the cabbage. It pulled the leaves and grass and little bird feathers over itself, and because of the Fall and the cold and the wind, it went under.

Soon after the toad had gone under, the wind blew all the leaves from the tree that grew before Jim's bedroom window. After it had blown the leaves down, the wind chased the leaves all over the yard. The wind whistled around the garage, blew up against the big sign, and piled up the leaves against the stretched chicken wire. The wind blew so hard through the chicken wire, it blew the big cabbage down. The green-ball head of the cabbage tipped down from its stem, and bent to the ground.

THE TIME HAD COME

In the cold afternoon of the windy day there was nobody in all the backyards, except Jim. But the neighbor put on his coat, and came out on his porch, and yelled out above the wind, "Jim, Jim—can you hear me? The time has come for the harvest. The time has come to take up your cabbage. You did grow a prize cabbage, didn't you, Jim? Look at that—it toppled right over from its own great weight!"

It was no use to shout up against the wind to the neighbor. Jim just smiled, and waved, and nodded his head.

The neighbor knew, but Jim also knew that the time had come to take up the cabbage. Jim had known it from the butterflies, and from the wrens, and from the rabbit that had gone away. He knew it from the snail and from the toad that had gone under. In their way they had all told him, "Jim, the time has come for the harvest."

46

In the cold wind in the garden among the blowing leaves Jim began to tug at his cabbage. But the cabbage had grown so deep, with such a thick stem and spread-out roots, that for all of Jim's tugging it would not let go from the ground in which it had grown so long.

In the wind and cold and with the leaves blowing, Jim tugged. Suddenly the deep roots in the ground let go. Jim staggered back so hard with the big cabbage, he sat down hard against the big sign. There lay the cabbage, there sat Jim, but there still stood the sign. The sign still said:

JIM JORDAN'S VEGETABLE GARDEN

But now the time had come to take up the sign. Jim let the big cabbage wait while first he pulled up the sign, and carried it into the garage for the winter. He set the sign against the wall next to his brother Harold's saw.

Then Jim went back to the cabbage in his garden. Just as he was struggling the big cabbage up against his chest to carry it into the house, his mother came out on the porch, and called out into the wind, "Jim, come in the house now. It's too cold and windy outside, and it's almost supper time."

With the big cabbage hugged against his chest, Jim could not answer his mother. He could not even come. He couldn't walk with the big cabbage—the stem and the spreading roots got in the way of his legs. He could not hold the cabbage, it was so big and round he could not get his arms around it far enough—his fingers wouldn't touch. He had to let it down to the ground again.

He hurried to the garage. He got his brother Harold's saw. He sawed the thick stem of the cabbage right below the big, round head of the cabbage.

Just as Jim was sawing with Harold's saw, his big brother, Harold, came out on the porch, and yelled into the wind, "JIM! Didn't you hear Mother? You come this minute."

Jim could not answer Harold—not when he was sawing a cabbage with his big brother's saw!

At last he sawed right through the stem. He carried the thick stem with all its roots to the spot where the cabbage had grown—to give the stem and the roots back to the ground that had grown the cabbage. But there was a big, disturbed hole where the stem and the roots had come up from the ground. The cold toad stirred under the leaves at the edge of the hole. The wren nest lay tipped over. The silver snail slept stiff and cold.

At that moment Jim's sister, Julia, called. She hardly poked her head out of the door, and she just called one call, "Come on now, Jim, we're waiting!"

Jim could not listen and could not come—not with the toad and snail disturbed and cold! He hurried back to the cabbage, he pulled all the outer leaves off the great, green ball of cabbage. He laid them over the snail and toad for a snug bed to tuck them in from the cold. He laid the thick stem with all its roots on top of the bed of cabbage leaves, so that the wind could not blow the leaves away from the snail and the toad. But the stem and the roots could not hold down all the cabbage leaves—the cold wind tugged at them and blew them up.

Jim hurried to the garage with his brother Harold's saw. He put it back in its place next to the big sign. Then he picked up the sign, and carried it back to the garden. He laid it face down to hold the cabbage leaves down that were over the toad and the snail. And there lay the sign, still saying face down—as if to the toad and the sleeping snail:

JIM JORDAN'S VEGETABLE GARDEN

Then Jim was ready to take up his cabbage and carry it into the house. Just as he picked up the great, green ball that was now the whole cabbage, just as he struggled it up to his chest and hugged it against his chest—Jim's father came out of the house. And he bellowed out above the wind, "JIM. This is the last call. The whole family is sitting around the supper table just waiting for you. So it's right now, and this minute! AND HURRY."

That minute Jim came—and hurried. But even with all the outer leaves given to the snail and the toad, the cabbage was still so big and round, Jim's arms could not go around it—his fingers wouldn't touch.

Jim could not even look over the cabbage to see where the porch steps were when he went up the back porch. He could not see the bottom of the door over the big cabbage, so he kicked the door. The door banged, and Jim yelled, "Let me in. Let me in."

In the house they thought something was wrong with Jim, and they all came running. Sister Julia threw open the door, but then she threw up her hands, and screamed, "WHERE in the WORLD did you get that BIG cabbage?"

And Harold yelled, "Look at that big monster of a cabbage." And Jim's mother clapped her astonished hands together and exclaimed, "In all my life I never saw such a beautiful cabbage."

Jim's father didn't exclaim, didn't yell and ask questions. He pushed everybody aside, took the big cabbage out of Jim's arms, and carried it into the house for him. He carried it to the dining room table that was all set for supper. He put the cabbage on the table right in the center of everything. There was the cabbage—huge and big and green and glossy and beautiful.

For once around the supper table they didn't talk and talk, and guess and guess, and ask each other questions. They all sat looking at the cabbage. They looked at the cabbage, and Jim smiled and looked at them—and at the big cabbage.

There under the lamp light on the table lay the cabbage—so big, so huge, so beautiful and glossy green with lamp light—so almost hard to believe, that in a soft voice of surprise Jim had to tell them all, "I grew it in my garden."

And everybody looked at Jim—and at the beautiful cabbage.

80312

Set in Janson
Format by Gertrude Awe
Typography by Haddon Craftsmen
Printed by Murray Printing Co.
Bound by Haddon Bindery
Published by Harper & Row, Publishers, Incorporated,